For Jason ~ N.C.

LITTLE TIGER PRESS
An imprint of Magi Publications
1 The Coda Centre, 189 Munster Road, London SW6 6AW
www.littletigerpress.com

First published in Great Britain 2010
This edition published 2011

Text and illustrations copyright © Natalie Chivers 2010
Natalie Chivers has asserted her right to be identified
as the author and illustrator of this work under
the Copyright, Designs and Patents Act, 1988

A CIP catalogue record for this book is available from the British Library

ISBN 978-1-84895-021-4

Printed in China • LTP/1800/0140/0910

2 4 6 8 10 9 7 5 3 1

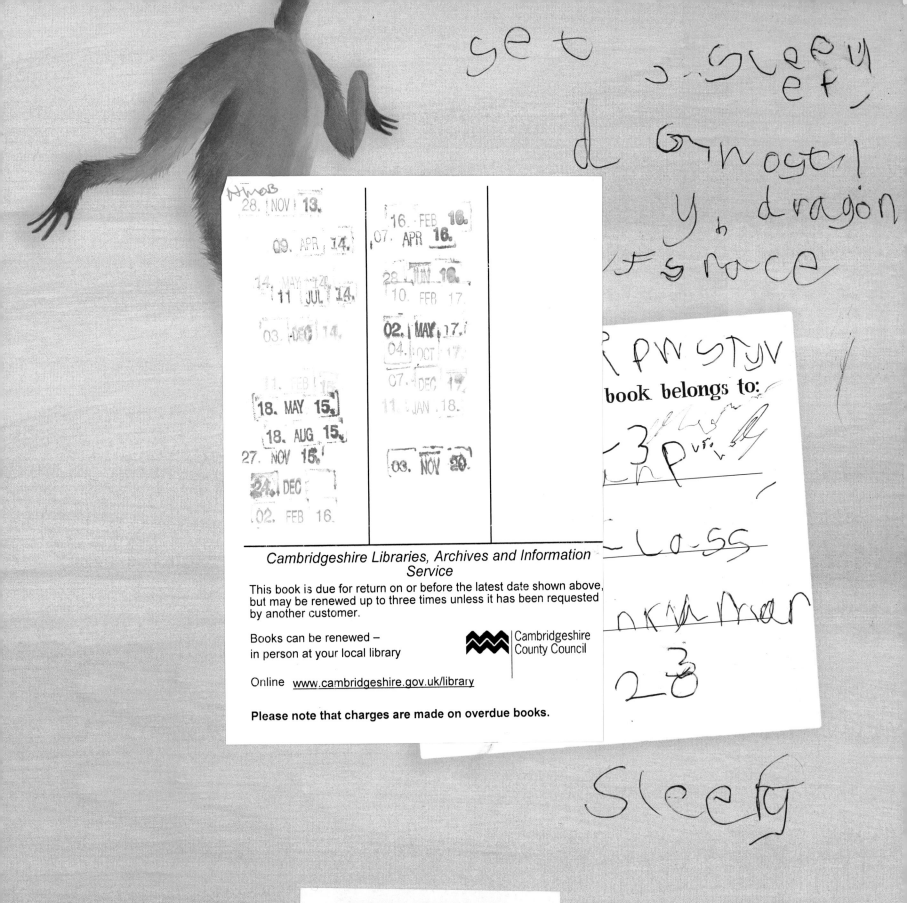

Natalie Chivers

Rhino's Great BIG Itch!

LITTLE TIGER PRESS
London

Rhino had an itch – a great **big terrible itch,** right in his ear.

He twisted . . .

he turned . . .

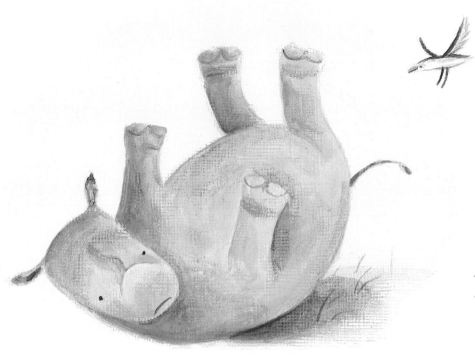

he wriggled,
he rolled . . .

But the itch just
wouldn't go.

"All you need is a little help!" said Bird.

"You're right!" said Rhino. So . . .

. . . off he went to find someone
to scratch his itch.

"Can **YOU** scratch my itch, Frog?"
Rhino asked.

But Frog was
too slimy.

Monkey was too silly.

Lizard was too **prickly.**

And Rhino didn't even bother
to ask Lion!

It was no good.
The itch was still there.

"All I need is a little help!"
Rhino sighed.

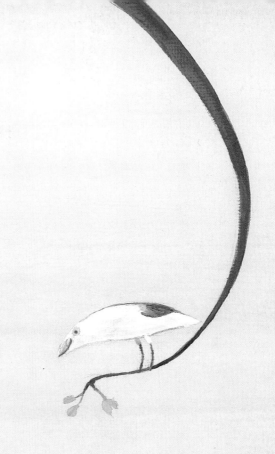

"I can help!"
said a little voice.

"How can **you** help, Bird?" asked Rhino.
"My itch is **big,** and you are far too tiny."

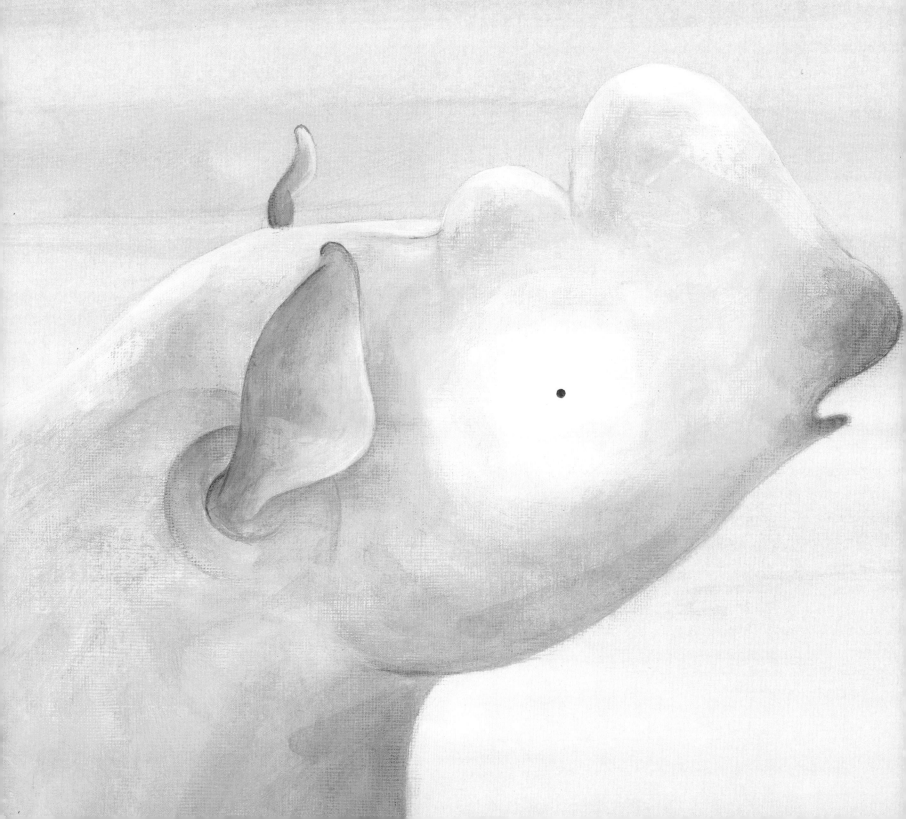

"I may be small," said Bird,
"but I am **just right** for you!"

So with
a hop . . .

and a skip . . .

and a little peck . . .

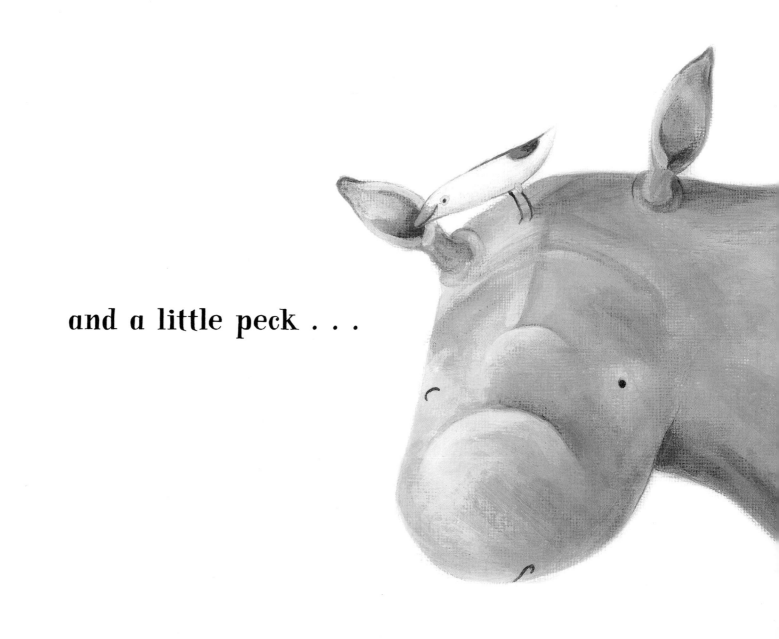

. . . the itch was gone!

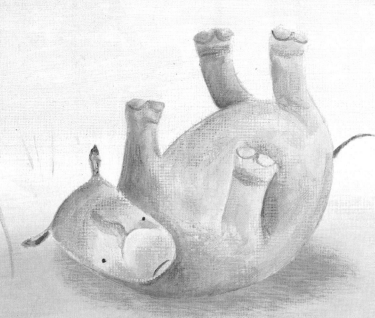
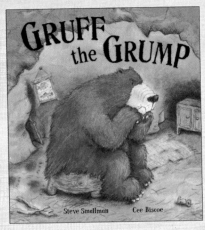

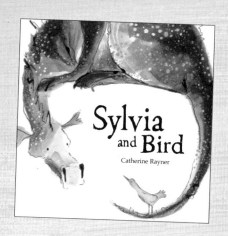